Stephanie Helber

W0414561

Heroes of the underwater forest

With illustrations by Paula Senff

Stephanie Helber

Heroes of the underwater forest

With illustrations by Paula Senff

ISENSEE VERLAG
OLDENBURG

We would like to sincerely thank the Institute for Chemistry and Biology of the Marine Environment at the Carl von Ossietzky University of Oldenburg for its support.

Texts: Stephanie Helber

Illustrations: Paula Senff

Typesetting and design: Stefanie Tegeler, Isensee Verlag

Bibliografische Information Der Deutschen Bibliothek

Die Deutsche Nationalbibliothek verzeichnet diese Publikation in der Deutschen Nationalbibliografie; detaillierte bibliografische Daten sind im Internet über http://dnb.d-nb.de abrufbar.

ISBN 978-3-7308-1885-5

Gedruckt bei Isensee in Oldenburg

STEPHANIE HELBER grew up in a village in the Black Forest, Germany. Since she was little, she loved to dive in the ocean - her second home. Officially, she is working at the ICBM as a marine biologist, investigating seagrass meadows, tropical coral reefs, but also colorful reefs right in front of our doorsteps in the North Sea. In reality, she is probably off on her next adventure, busy making new friends underwater.

Photo: Sergey Savenko

Stephanie Helber

PAULA SENFF always liked to paint. As a child she was rather afraid of the ocean, but that changed quickly once she was able to dive and look beneath the surface. She works as a biologist and studies the creatures under water. With her illustrations she wants to inspire others to love and protect them.

Paula Senff

Chloe gazes at a picture in her living room. It shows her together with her friends, her mom and her mom's colleagues. They are all gathered around a big glass aquarium filled with seawater. Through the glass you can see flowerpots with small, green leaves peeking out.

"Flowers underwater?" you might wonder. What is this about?...

Chloe had moved with her mom Fay to an exotic place, called Zanzibar. It is a beautiful island of palm trees surrounded by clear, blue waters off the East African coast.

Fay is a marine biologist and travelled with Chloe to Zanzibar to study together with her colleague and friend Fahima everything that lives in the ocean. Fahima has a son the same age as Chloe. His name is Amo.

Chloe had never seen the sea before. She could swim, but was both excited and afraid to go into the unknown blue ocean.

Amo took her hand into his, smiled at her and said: "Let's go in together!"

They were having fun playing in the water, when suddenly something touched Chloe's foot and she started screaming.
"What happened?", asked Amo.
"I don't know. Something touched my foot. I didn't like it. It was scary", replied Chloe.
"Don't be afraid!", said an unknown voice behind them. Both turned around and looked into the gentle eyes of an animal that they had never seen before. It looked like a cow, but with flippers instead of legs and a tail resembling a whale's. Its grey, leathery skin reminded Amo of the skin of an elephant he had seen before. "Are you a sea elephant?"
The strange looking animal started laughing. "No, I am a dugong – a sea cow ... But you are not so far off. My closest relatives are the elephants, but I prefer to live in the sea."
"What is your name?", asked Chloe.
"My name is Nya", answered the dugong. "And I want to be your friend. I am quite lonely here."
"Where do you come from?", asked Amo burning with curiosity.

"Come with me, I will show you", replied Nya and disappeared slowly into the water.
"Should we follow her?", asked Chloe a bit anxiously, but Amo was already diving down. Chloe did not want to be left behind and followed the two of them hesitantly.

After swimming for a while, they suddenly saw a huge underwater forest. Green, thick leaves as far as the eye could see, swaying with the rhythm of the waves. Small fishes were darting through the leaves like butterflies flying in between blades of grass. As they swam along, they spotted all kinds of colourful animals, such as starfish, sea urchins and even a seahorse.
"Here is where I live", said Nya.
"Wow, it is so beautiful here. Are these small trees?", asked Chloe.

"No", said Mr. Dolphin as he passed by. "These are flowers. I am just picking some for my wife."

"Flowers?" asked Chloe doubtfully.
"I can't see any colourful blooms."

Mr. Dolphin gently wrapped his fin around Chloe showing her a fragile, white flower in between all the green leaves.

"Over 100 million years ago, the ancestors of these flowers grew on land before they went back into the sea. All of this happened when there were still dinosaurs."

They ran back home, excited to tell their moms about their adventures. "Oh, you discovered the seagrass meadow?", asked Fay.

"Yes, it is beautiful", answered Chloe. "We made a new friend, too. Her name is Nya and she is a dugong."

"Maybe you were playing with the same dugong as I once did as a child", said Fahima.

"No, mom, you are too old!", said Amo.

"Thank you that is very nice young man", replied Fahima. Everybody started laughing. "Did you know that dugongs can live almost as long as people do? Some can even live to be 70 years old. That is as old as your grandma, Amo."

Chloe and Amo played with their new friend Nya in the seagrass meadow every day. There was so much to discover!

"Bye, see you tomorrow, Nya", said Amo after another day of adventures. He and Chloe were swimming back to the beach. Amo was the better swimmer and Chloe could not keep up with him. Suddenly, she felt something bumping against her leg. When she turned around, she looked into a wide open mouth. It had giant teeth. The front teeth looked like those of a rabbit, but more massive and mean.

"What are you doing, trigger?", shouted Nya. "They are my friends."
"Oh, I am really sorry", replied the giant triggerfish-mom, "but they were swimming right above my nest and I thought they wanted to eat my babies. Look, here."
The triggerfish-mom pointed with her fin towards a round hole in the sand. In the middle was a clutch of tiny eggs - so tiny, you could barely see them.
"Thank you, Nya!", said Chloe and took her friend into her arms. "You saved me."

"Come let's go to the beach together", said Fahima.

As the four of them were walking along the beach, Amo felt suddenly something hard below his foot. He looked down and picked up a small, green ball.

"Oh, that's great, you found a seagrass fruit", said Fahima.

"This green ball?" asked Amo surprised.

"Seagrasses grow from seeds just as flowers do", explained Fay. "At certain times of the year we can find their seeds at the beach. The seeds of seagrasses are protected within the fruit.

The fruit is the green ball you discovered at the beach, Amo.

An apple tree also produces fruits – the apples. Inside you have the apple seeds. Seagrasses do the same", explained Fahima and opened the fruit. "Here, look! Inside each fruit are two to three seeds."

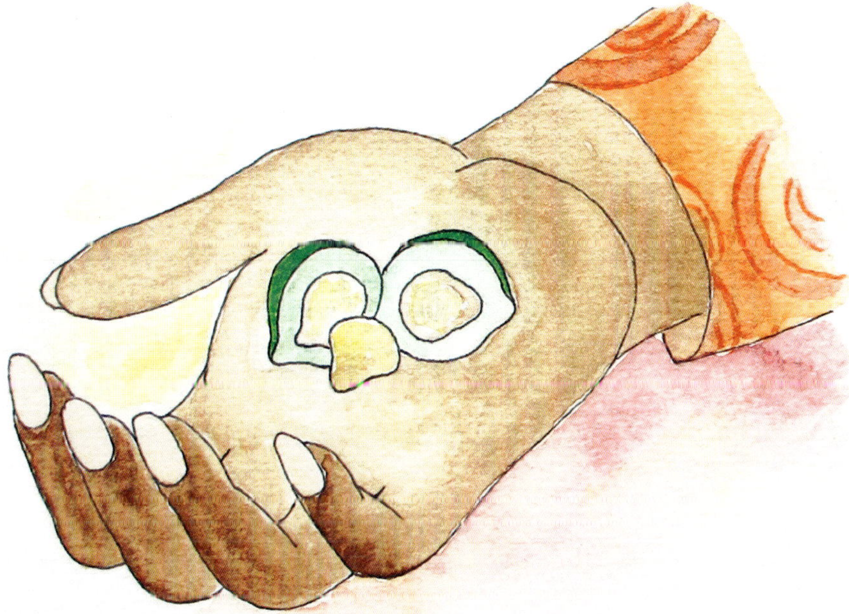

"They look like the seeds in our lemons at home", exclaimed Amo surprised.

Then summer came and it got very hot. The sun was burning. The heat was unbearable. Chloe and Amo did not want to move, let alone go to the beach.
"You two haven't been swimming at the beach in days", said Fay.
"It is too hot. When I go out, I start sweating right away. I don't like it", replied Chloe.
"Yes", agreed Amo. "It is too hot to move. Even the water is too hot to cool down."

Finally, summer came to an end and it started getting cooler. Chloe and Amo went back to the beach. A lot had changed. A big hotel had been built right at the beach. When they entered the water, they could not find their friend Nya anywhere. The water looked very different.

They swam to Nya's home. Where they once could find a green underwater forest, there was nothing but sand with slimy green algae growing in some places. It looked like a desert. The colourful underwater forest was gone and with it all its animals. Both of them were shocked and started crying.

"What happened here?", asked Chloe in despair.

"We have to find out and make sure Nya is OK", said Amo.

Amo spotted something shiny on the sea floor. It looked like a metal pipe with a small dolphin figurine at the end.

Suddenly, they heard rumbling and gurgling noises. Both turned around. Out of the mouth of this beautiful metal dolphin came a thick, brown-blackish liquid. This liquid smelled like rotten eggs and pee.
"Ew, gross!!! Where is this coming from?", asked Amo.
They gazed to the beach and realized that the pipe was leading up to the newly built hotel.

At home, Fay and Fahima told them that this disgusting smelling liquid is what you flush down the toilet.
"They put poo into the ocean?", asked Chloe surprised.

"Yes, unfortunately some hotels do this, although this is actually strictly forbidden", explained Fahima. "People swimming in the ocean can get very sick and it is also bad for the seagrass meadows. That is for sure one reason why the underwater forest has disappeared." Fahima and Fay talked to the hotel owner and could convince him to stop piping the hotel's waste into the ocean.

It was only a small success. Weeks went by, but the underwater forest did not return. Only the dead desert remained. Chloe and Amo felt completely discouraged.

"Just like you two, the seagrasses also do not like hot summers. If it gets too hot or the water is polluted, they will die. Once they are dead, it is difficult to bring this underwater forest back to life again", said Fay.

Was the underwater forest gone forever? What happened to Nya? Would they ever see their friend again? How could they help?

„I have an idea", said Chloe. „Let's go and search for the seagrass fruits at the beach."
Together, Chloe and Amo walked to the beach and collected hundreds of seagrass fruits.

Chloe walked into the water, took sand from the sea floor and filled it into a flowerpot. She opened a seagrass fruit and carefully placed one of their collected seeds into the sand.
„Come on, help me, Amo! We still have a lot to do."
Both looked at the seemingly endless row of empty flowerpots.

The whole day they planted all of their collected seeds like flowers into the small flowerpots. They placed the flowerpots in a big glass aquarium filled with seawater.

"That looks funny. Like a garden, but then underwater", said Amo joyfully.

They had to wait four months – it felt like an eternity. Then the seagrasses started to grow. Small, green leaves were peeking out of the flowerpots.

They proudly showed their moms what they achieved together.
"That is incredible", said Fay amazed.
"Now, you only need to wait a bit longer so that the roots of the seagrasses get strong enough to protect them from currents and waves", said Fahima.

Finally the day had come. Amo and Chloe gathered all their friends to help plant their little seagrass babies into the ocean.
It was a big event. People from the villages and tourists came to the beach, curious to see what was happening.

After a few weeks, they noticed that the water was getting clear again. Amo could see to the bottom of the ocean. Life started to return to their newly planted baby-forest. Chloe and Amo could observe how small fishes, crabs and even an octopus settled into their new home. It was a great success!

Chloe and Amo went swimming every day to see how their baby- plants were doing. Their leaves started to grow and they were getting thicker and thicker.

Soon they were not babies anymore – they were full-grown seagrasses. The underwater forest was back.

Finally, they also met Nya again. "Nya, we missed you so much", exclaimed Chloe, hugging their lost friend.
"My home was destroyed, I had nothing to eat so I had to leave", explained Nya, "but how is the seagrass back?", she asked surprised. "I thought that I had lost my home forever."

"We planted a new seagrass meadow just for you, Nya", explained Amo bursting with pride.
"Wow, I cannot believe you two did all of this. This is amazing!" said Nya beaming, overjoyed to have her home and her friends back.